from the creators of the Black Lagoon series

MISSION TRIP IMPOSSIBLE

written by **Mike Thaler**   illustrated by **Jared Lee**

ZONDERVAN.com/
AUTHORTRACKER
follow your favorite authors

To Betsy, a believer who believed
—M.T.

To Lynn Steinkirchner
—J.L.

ZONDERkidz

Mission Trip Impossible
Copyright © 2009 by Mike Thaler
Illustrations © 2009 by Jared Lee Studio, Inc.

Requests for information should be addressed to:
Zonderkidz, *Grand Rapids, Michigan 49530*

Library of Congress Cataloging-in-Publication Data

Thaler, Mike, 1936-
  Mission trip impossible / by Mike Thaler ; illustrated by Jared Lee.
      p. cm. -- (Tales from the back pew)
  ISBN 978-0-310-71590-0 (softcover)
  [1. Missions--Fiction. 2. Christian life--Fiction.] I. Lee, Jared D., ill. II. Title.
  PZ7.T3Mj 2009

  [E]--dc22   2008007599

All Scripture quotations unless otherwise noted are taken from the *Holy Bible: New International Version*®. NIV®. Copyright © 1973, 1978, 1984 by International Bible Society. Used by permission of Zondervan. All rights reserved.

All rights reserved. No part of this publication may be reproduced, stored in a retrieval system, or transmitted in any form or by any means—electronic, mechanical, photocopy, recording, or any other—except for brief quotations in printed reviews, without the prior permission of the publisher.

Zonderkidz is a trademark of Zondervan.

Editor: Betsy Flikkema
Art Director & Design: Merit Alderink

Printed in China

09 10 11 12 • 5 4 3 2 1

Our church is going on a mission trip tomorrow.

I heard all about mission trips. This is one trip I want to be *missin'*. They search the world for the worst places they can find ... the more dangerous the better.

If there are jungles filled with wild animals that can eat you ... even better.

 Poisonous snakes, insects, and deadly plants are great! Fatal diseases rate high.

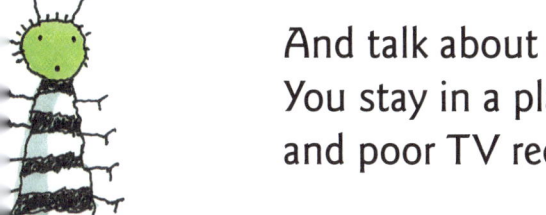

And talk about uncomfortable!
You stay in a place with no roof, no hot water,
and poor TV reception. No thanks.

Sometimes you bring hungry folks food, but *you* wind up on the menu.

Those folks are called cannibals because they *can-nibble* on you.

They love to have missionaries over for dinner.
It's called a potluck. You're in the *pot*, and you're out of *luck*.

If you try to run away, they just call you *fast food*.
I'll skip dinner, thank you.

Then there's the weather. You have to go to the hottest places in the summer and the coldest places in the winter.

It's either wheeze or freeze. No air conditioner ... no air!

I think about the mission trip of the apostle Paul. He was stoned.

Put in jail.

Shipwrecked.

And bitten by a deadly snake.
The other apostles didn't have it easy either.

And why? Why do they go? To tell people about Jesus.
Can't I just write them a letter or send them an email?

I like places with sidewalks and toy stores.

Can't we go to Disney World and tell them about Jesus?

Well, I'll go anyway. Knowing Jesus has changed my life so much, I want to tell other people that He can change theirs too. So I get up early in the morning (suffer, suffer), and Mom drives me to the church parking lot.

All the kids are there, and we get on a bus. We sing songs and nibble on donuts as we drive to a jungle or a desert.

Hey, we only drive twenty minutes and stop on the other side of town.

All the houses have roofs, and there's even a Pizza Mutt on the corner—civilization. This is promising.

"I'M HUNGRY, CAPTAIN. CAN WE LAND?"

"GOOD IDEA."

We get out and sing more songs, do puppet shows, and hand out toys. Hey, this is cool! And I don't see any wild animals.

For lunch, we treat everyone to fast food.
(I wore my sneakers, just in case.)

The kids are so grateful and friendly
that I'm really sorry we have to leave so soon.

Hey, I'm coming back next week to visit all my new friends and tell them more about my best friend, Jesus.

Go into all the world and preach the good news to all creation.
—Mark 16:15